SUMMER MELOD'

by Anushree Nande

abuddhapress@yahoo.com

®™©2021

ISBN: 9798472077255

To Suhas Aaji and Kishor Aajoba, rockstar grandparents, with all my love.

Author's note:

This is a story I first started to tell in 2011 during the third and last year of my bachelor's degree. Back then, it looked and felt very different—the polished version that became my submission for the final project, and even the version that was my dissertation for the resultant master's.

Over the next couple of years, even after I felt like I finally had a grip on the characters and the story I wanted to tell, it never seemed to come together like I wanted it to. I kept putting it away but it never fully left me and I'd always return; I didn't know whether it was belief that this was still a story I wanted to tell and I would, or the sheer, perhaps stubborn and sometimes frantic, determination not to let the time and energy I'd spent in this world go to waste that kept pulling me back to those typed pages and the years of accumulated handwritten notes. Underneath, there was always the question of whether this story was just a pipe dream and whether the block I felt whenever I even tried to start a new, longer work was something my mind had conjured up in its desperation to see this project through. Then, during some of the toughest months of an already tumultuous year, personally and with the pandemic, through the uncertainty and limbo and self-doubt at its peak, I had an inexplicable breakthrough with the narrative that changed everything.

A novel that was always a novelette; the story and characters I would never have been able to write when I first started, but were what they were always destined to be, which meant that I was meant to be where I was, *who* I was, meant to have lived through the growth and experiences of the past decade, to be able to write the version you're about to read. The version it always was.

Without further ado, here is *Summer Melody*.

It was still dark when Sophie started playing the Vivaldi. She kept her eyes closed, bow flying through Mendelssohn and Haydn, submerging her worries, each note taking turns at holding them down before tossing to the one after. The morning grew warmer amidst the first strains of Bach. Sophie played on until the faint sound of *his* cello started up somewhere out there in the drifts of her mind; she almost leaned into it by habit before jerking open her eyes, her bow stilled.

One of the windows in her tiny London studio overlooked a school, the low buildings unimaginatively placed in the middle of a standard-issue space. At Trinity, her room had overlooked a stone fountain in a small park that was mostly empty but for the old man who came every day and sat on the bench for an hour, no matter the weather. He would read his paper, sometimes a book, eat a snack, or just sit there facing the cracked, empty bowl of the fountain.

Sophie sighed and stood up, packing everything away. Her phone vibrated underneath her violin case.

Are you still coming to dinner tonight? Mum x

Despite telling April that she would know it was her, Sophie's mother insisted on signing off on all her texts. Today, she found it endearing, before remembering she still hadn't told her parents about the concert; posters had already started appearing at the usual places and it was only a matter of time before they found out. She hadn't even told Robby yet, though her best friend had been back from Vienna for more than a week now. But it felt selfish to want him all to herself when his mother needed him more. Sophie headed to the other side of the room to put the kettle on, careful to avoid the invitation crammed under a pile of junk mail on the narrow table she used for bits and bobs. But the carefully worded note in Paul's loopy handwriting followed her, just a couple of steps behind.

*

Sophie first met Paul Clark on the day she turned nineteen, late in her first semester at Trinity. It was a week after the college's winter concert, where he had performed Bach's

Cello Suite in G Major better than several professionals she'd heard. Here was a 21 year old going places, and sure enough, their director had made a special announcement that Paul was moving to Philadelphia after securing a coveted place on the exceedingly competitive Curtis Post-Baccalaureate Diploma programme. Sophie had felt a twinge she recognised as jealousy. An irrational jealousy that she wasn't a part of his life, he who played music that tunnelled into the spaces underneath her doubts and rendered them insignificant.

But here he was bumping into her at a local coffee place many Trinity students liked to frequent. He was standing right behind her in the line when she spun around to see if any of her friends were there; she hated sitting alone. As she turned, she brushed against him, knocking a folder out of his hand. A few loose pages fluttered out. Sophie instinctively bent down and gathered the ones within reach; looking up at him only once she had stood back up and handed them over to him.

Those grey-blue eyes were intense, but friendly. He looked so serious, so put together, so damn sure of his place in the world. Even at the concert, she'd wondered how he was only two years older than her. But then he started playing and all else was forgotten.

"Your performance at the winter concert was my favourite of the night."

Sophie cringed inwardly. She was still waiting for her change, half-turned towards him. But the next moment, she was rewarded with a shy smile that was endearing in its contrast to the absolute confidence of his playing.

"That's very kind. Thank you."

"Your father was in the Rizzoni Quartet, wasn't he?"

Paul had already put his hand in his pocket for his wallet, in anticipation of being next in line. He looked up at Sophie's question and something like surprise passed across his face. She looked at her feet. Why had she asked a question she knew the answer to? Damn her need to keep this conversation going. Sophie was about to swivel back around to see where the barista was when Paul spoke again. This time, there was something in the tone that made her glance up and hold his gaze.

"I wouldn't have thought that many people from our generation would know who they were...who he was."

"My mother used to play their music on the days my father was out of town on one of his conferences. She didn't say it out loud, but I think they made her tolerate the long hours I made her play with me and my dolls."

This was far from the poised conversations she'd staged in her mind since the concert. But it drew a real smile from him, one that Sophie hadn't dared to hope for, even in her daydreams. It was just the beginning.

Now, on the Tube to her parents', Sophie nudged all unwanted Paul thoughts under her seat, placing her palms flat on her knees, as if that would keep everything in place. She snuck a look around the busy carriage to see if anyone had noticed. Just then, they pulled into the next stop and the person standing across from her got off, exposing a small square of the window. With her slight frame, brown hair flecked with dark gold, oval face and wide-set brown eyes, Sophie looked like neither of her parents. As a kid, she took it personally, looking nothing like her mother. In her rebel teenage years, it was as a matter of pride, a badge of her uniqueness. Now in her twenties, Sophie was undecided. Call it a sort of uneasy truce. She swallowed the tears suddenly built up in her throat as the train slowed down at Raynes Park and she got off.

*

"I was hoping Robby and Lydia could join us for dessert, but she called to say she was too tired."

It was after dinner, and for the past hour and a half, Sophie had been wondering how to bring up the concert. James was reminiscing about the good old days when he and April lived in Japan and it suited Sophie to be enveloped in memories that felt like they were hers. At this moment, her father was over at the record player in the corner of the living room. It was still raining, the sky flashing and darkening, and her parents had decided that she should stay over. April was in

16

the kitchen, loading the dishwasher, which she wouldn't turn on until much later, when the music had faded away.

If there was one genre her parents agreed on, it was jazz. James was fond enough of classical, but that was only because he couldn't quite avoid that, what with first his wife and then his daughter choosing to play it. April, Sophie was well aware, only tolerated her father listening to his rock vinyls as long as she was in a different room, preferably soundproof. But it was jazz that still connected them, even after all this time. Ella Fitzgerald and Dizzy Gillespie and Duke Ellington. It was to a jazz club that James had taken her to on their first date in Tokyo; they'd explored other places and local artists over dates spanning the year and a half they'd both stayed until they decided to get married and move back to London.

"I'm hoping to meet him for lunch later this week. I think it'll do him good to get out of the house a little but I don't blame him for not wanting to."

Neither of them needed to spell out how close he was to his mother or how guilty he now felt for moving away a few years ago. Sophie burrowed into the soft throw she'd pulled around her shoulders. She was on the floor, her back to the couch.

"I asked the caregiver who said Lydia might be strong enough to spend the day out soon, so maybe we can coordinate. That way Robby won't mind leaving her for a bit."

Her mother returned from the kitchen with homemade frozen yoghurt. It was Lydia's favourite and April made it a point to take some over every week, especially now.

"You should take her to that garden she loves." Sophie accepted a bowl from her mother.

"That's a great idea. Also, I wanted to ask if you'd like to come shopping with me tomorrow. I have a few things I need to buy and would love the company. When was the last time we did something together?" That last line was almost murmured, part of a private conversation. April paused, a beat longer than needed, before going around Sophie and sitting down on the couch, her legs pulled up. "Unless you already have plans. I know it's the weekend."

Sophie glanced at her, feeling guilty at how worried her mother sounded that she'd say no. She took a bite of the yoghurt—tiny pieces of blueberry cold against her tongue—before the guilt made her say something she couldn't reel back in.

"I'd love to, Mum."

She felt her mother's smile on the back of her head and was irrationally glad that April had chosen not to get into any difficult conversations tonight.

James walked over and settled next to April as the opening strains of Ella swirled through the living room. In Sophie's peripheral vision, she saw her parents lean against each other. Ella was singing about young love and how its texture was so unique to anything else that comes much later. Its innocence, its passion, its sincerity. She was wrong about the innocence, Sophie thought. First loves rammed under the best of intentions and scattered everything until it was hard to know what, where, how and why. For Sophie, it was music, a fatigued reason if there ever was one, but Paul remained an inseparable part of the same music. Even more than two years after parting ways.

Sophie took another bite of the dessert, which was still deliciously cool but softer, more pliable. She glanced at her parents again, this time her head tilted to the side. Her mother didn't look her age. That night she had on a bottle-green jumper over black trousers, her dark brown, almost black, hair worn back in a simple ponytail. James had short greying hair he still cut himself, but it was his eyes you noticed first—the flecks of gold and hazel in the dark brown—and the laugh lines around them and his mouth that he claimed he was born with. In that soft light, Sophie had a sudden vision of April at her age. She shifted so that the top of her back touched her mother's knees. Ella Fitzgerald crooned on, more contemplative now. The three of them listened in silence, the rain tapping against the house.

*

It was disorienting to be back in her old room and bed, swaddled in the citrusy scent of the only detergent April had

20

ever used. Sophie breathed it in just as daybreak spilled in through the gaps in the curtains. Robby had texted deep into the night.

Lunch in the week sounds great - alright if it's a bit last minute? Mum is doing better though x

Sure, just let me know. I'm not teaching any afternoons this week. Glad she's doing better. Mum said something about taking her out this week so maybe we can work with that. Can't wait to see you :) x

The rain hadn't stopped, only now it felt more like a duty than the want and urgency that pounded the windows of the house the night before. It lulled Sophie back into a dreamless sleep. She woke up to her parents moving around and making breakfast downstairs, something that took her back to weekend mornings during the school year. Sophie sat up and rubbed her eyes. If she closed them, she could almost imagine being eight years old again, excited by the possibilities the weekend held.

She smiled, her hand reaching for her phone, expecting a message back from Robby. Instead, there was an email from an old Trinity friend.

*

"You should wear scarves more often, you'd pull off most colours with that hair and those eyes." April paused at a display of folded fabric, colour-coded and set inches apart from each other. Today, she wore a deep gauzy green shot through with pale gold threads.

"They're restrictive enough when it's cold." Sophie placed her hand on a particularly bright orange and felt its cool, slippery touch. "This one would suit you though."

"I've already got three in similar shades. I'd really love to buy you one, Soph. There are some lovely options over at that boutique near yours, if you don't like anything here." When Sophie looked confused, she added, "You know, the one by that little florist's shop?"

"How is it that you know more about my neighbourhood than I do?" Sophie laughed, surprised at herself. Normally, she would have been annoyed that April knew something she didn't. "When did you go there, anyway?"

"The time I dropped off some of your clothes. It was a nice day, so I decided to walk around and came across that lovely lady who owns the florist's. She wasn't that busy and we got to talking and she told me about her neighbour, who had recently set up a boutique, and was having a sort of exhibition. I didn't have enough time but promised her that I would be back."

Who was this woman who made friends with florists and boutique owners? Sophie thought about how little she knew her mother and how little she had allowed her mother to know her. "Maybe I can come with you. How about Wednesday after I finish teaching?" She pinched the rising tide of emotions before they caused real damage.

"I'd love that." April smiled. They walked over to the men's section since her mother never could go anywhere without buying James a little something. They were looking at ties—the brighter the better—when April glanced at Sophie, who was next to her.

"Are you doing okay, honey?" There was something in her voice that made Sophie look up. Concern, and almost, well, *tenderness*.

"What do you mean?" Her throat burned with the sudden effort to keep it from closing in on itself.

"You have that look you do when you're trying to fight something on your own. I know you don't like anyone else to meddle, especially not me, but I wanted to let you know that I'm still here." April looked at her daughter again, this time her gaze held.

Sophie suddenly wanted to tell her everything—Paul returning to London for a concert and inviting her, writing that it would be nice to see her, what April thought she should do about her Trinity friend keen to have her audition for their up-and-coming quartet; underneath it all was the question that had been plaguing her since the day she'd overhead she may be the reason April stopped performing. But the words wouldn't come, so she squeezed her mother's forearm and hoped it was enough for now. April covered her hand with hers and they stayed like that for a moment and another, until a voice dissipated the comfort.

"April? April Walters? That *is* you!"

The way her mother started at the woman whom the voice belonged to, Sophie was convinced they knew each other. But by the time April turned toward the woman, her face was tidied away.

"Oh, come on, I haven't changed that much! Or maybe I have, but shush," the woman giggled. Despite the air of frivolity that clouded around her, Sophie saw that she smiled with her eyes which were soft but bright. Dark, shiny shoulder-length hair with streaks of grey curled at her ears and her forehead. Sophie didn't remember ever seeing her.

"Madhuri, it's good to see you," April offered, finally. Her face was still tight, her voice frayed.

Madhuri beamed and turned to Sophie. "Is this your daughter?" She stuck out her right hand. Her wrist was bare except for a black thread with the knot facing up. "Your mother and I went to Trinity together. I haven't seen her since she disappeared off the face of the earth once you were born."

Sophie couldn't unravel the ball of sentiments in her tone and she didn't dare try.

"Yes, this is Sophie, my daughter. Soph, this is Madhuri. One of the most talented students in our year."

"You're one to talk." Madhuri turned to Sophie. "You don't need me to tell you how amazing your mum is, I bet you've heard all the stories until you're tired of them." She continued, "I miss living with her though, even now that I have a family that doesn't stifle me. Rillie was so much fun. I'm afraid I was a bit wild back then, still revelling in finally living away from home and all the rules." There was now a confiding air to the conversation.

"Rillie?"

"That was what my friends called me." April's voice was again a bit strained. She turned to Madhuri. "It's been good seeing you, but I'm afraid we're in a bit of a hurry. Why don't we get lunch sometime?"

"Well, now that I'm no longer performing, I have all the time in the world. Here's my card, it really would be nice to catch up, Ril." The look on her face suggested that she meant it, but was resigned to not hearing back from her old friend.

April put the card in her purse and reached out for a hug as if by habit before drawing back a little, but Madhuri was already leaning over the space between them. She then turned to Sophie and hugged her. When they separated, a wistful quality lay suspended in the air above their heads, spreading out beyond the bright lights of the departmental store.

April and Sophie watched Madhuri go down the escalator at the far end. April turned away before her daughter, her hands tracing the rows of cufflinks in front of her. Her face remained sad during the time it took them to make their purchase and walk to the Tube, making strained conversation about talking to Robby and Lydia for their plans in the week. Sophie hugged her mother goodbye, tighter than she usually

27

permitted herself; then watched her melt away into the afternoon crowds like she'd never existed, taking the earlier warmth with her.

*

Ever since the run-in with Madhuri, April seemed moodier. Sophie, craving the short-lived understanding between them, realised again how little she knew her mother and wondered whether she should ask James what to do. He was sure to have some ideas. Maybe she could swing by after her lunch with Robby. They had decided on a cafe in the neighbourhood. Sophie was excited to see her best friend after months. Video calls and texts weren't the same as being able to pop over next door for a chat. But now, in this space that neither of them could recognise after its renovation, it felt like they were continuing a long-paused conversation.

"No, Andy's the wise guy, Brian's the quiet one."

"And he's the one who still insists on calling you Miss W?" Robby grinned, pausing for a final mouthful of his cilantro rice and chicken. "I've been meaning to save that as your contact name in my phone."

Sophie rolled her eyes at him. They were debating what to share for dessert. April had texted that she and Lydia were having fun and wouldn't be home for a while yet. Robby still kept periodically checking his phone. When he did it just then, Sophie blurted out, "Paul's back."

Robby's head shot up, his fingers still hovering over his screen. She took a shallow breath and tried again.

"I mean, he isn't back, but he's going to be. His quartet is playing in London soon."

Robby put his phone to the side, waited.

"And that he'd like to see me if I wanted to meet. Oh and this quartet that a former Trinity classmate plays in wants me to audition as a replacement for their current second violinist who's stepping down."

Now that it was all out there, she felt relieved. Her best friend would tell her what to do. It was going to be okay.

"Wow, way to throw a guy off crumbled apple pie."
Robby smiled but she could tell he was thinking. Sophie
started to signal to the guy behind the counter before realising
that it had been a while since anyone here knew them or they
the staff. She nipped over to get the pie. When she was back,
Robby surveyed her with a look that told her she probably
wasn't going to like what he had to say.

"Okay, so, Paul. I may not have been here when you
two broke up but I remember all too well how wrecked you
were about it. You're in a better place but I'm not sure
meeting him won't do more harm than good." He hesitated;
instead, picking up the fork and spearing a small piece of
apple that had escaped the slice.

"And?" Sophie shored up her defences. "C'mon, Robby,
I'm not so fragile."

His face was resigned. "I don't think you're over him or
have accepted that you were the one who messed up." He
continued, "And to be very honest with you, Soph, I don't
think you can do any of that unless you allow yourself to

30

accept everything, well, everything with your mum and stop blaming all of your problems on her. I feel like it's the only way you're going to be able to move on." He sat up straighter; the words were out there, closing in on Sophie.

"Tell me how you really feel, Robby, won't you?"

She knew what she was about to say wasn't entirely the truth, but it was hard to let go of years of unresolved hurt. "And what's the point? I already know why she didn't want to teach me, have anything to do with my musical education. She hates me for what she had to give up, but she can't even be honest about it. Not like I even care anymore." Sophie hated how whiny she sounded, but she looked Robby in the eye, pushing back her tears, almost daring him to object.

He abruptly pushed his chair back and Sophie jumped.

"Oh, don't give me that—did you ever listen to her for more than two minutes when it came to your music? You were always busy defying everything anyone ever said because you were scared. Justifying your actions as some sort of necessary rebellion. I was the one caught in the crossfire between you and April and you and your frustration at the world. Did you ever once think of that?"

He signalled for the bill.

"You know what, Sophie? Be stubborn. I can be stubborn, too. Play your music, don't play your music. Talk to your mum or don't. Just don't keep complaining about it to me when you won't do anything to make it better."

Robby put some money down on the table and stood up. There were so many things Sophie wanted to say, but where do you start when you realise you've taken your best friend for granted and never realised it?

"Robby, please, where are you going?"

"Home to Mum." He walked towards the door, stopping before he opened it. He turned around. "If you didn't care, you wouldn't be so upset. You wouldn't still be trying to fix things. Think about that the next time you want to blame anyone or feel sorry for yourself."

*

You wouldn't still be trying to fix things. As time went by, Sophie had thought that she felt it lessen, the ever-present trace of *that* fight hanging over them like an inconvenient sprig of mistletoe. If April noticed it too, she never said. Then again, she hadn't said so much as a word about it since that day, not even by accident, like the words and thoughts that pushed and jostled at the edge of your attention, until they decided to take matters into their own hands.

There were some words that Sophie wished she could take back. Accusations that she knew, deep down, were unfair, but she wasn't ready to accept back then.

"Are you happy now?" Sophie had blasted into the silence, a few days after she'd broken up with Paul, out of sorts with everything and everyone around her, wanting someone to blame other than herself. Then, when April didn't respond, looked like she didn't know how to, or what to say, she had pushed further. "Isn't this what you wanted all along, for me to realise that I couldn't do this?"

April had flinched, but stayed silent. If Sophie had allowed herself to look at her mother, she might not have said what she did, might have seen something there that would've helped. But Sophie had pushed herself up and walked out into the hallway, not even bothering to slam the door. That night, after James came home from work, the three of them pretended that nothing was amiss, but the parents noticed that Sophie slipped away into her room as soon as the dishwasher was loaded, before the music started. The next day, she'd moved out.

Robby was already in Vienna for a few months by then, so for about a month and a half, she had camped over at the house of her closest Trinity friend, texting and talking with him every day but surrounding herself with Lia's family and the noise and chatter that comes with five people in one house and plenty coming and going at all times. She had sat with Lia's grandmother on their big sofa while the old woman pretended that she needed company in the form of an unemployed twenty year old. Sophie watched her soaps with

34

her, helped her sort through the fresh produce, read her parts of the newspaper while they waited for the food to cook. Even as the neighbours dropped in for a cuppa or for a chat. Even as she missed Paul and his quiet manner and hated herself for messing things up with him, though she wouldn't admit that to anyone.

Then, one morning, Sophie woke up and reached out to everyone she knew. She started composing jingles for adverts, got pulled into background scores for small, independent films. She put ads out for private violin tutorials. She also called her father and, after he'd promised not to say anything to April, asked for a loan to pay her first few months' rent on a studio that she had stumbled upon. James transferred the money, but not before telling her, in that quiet, non-pressure way of his, to at least call her mother if not come home for dinner. He would cook her favourite lasagne and they could all sit and talk calmly. He stressed the last word. April, he said, missed her, they both did, and they respected whatever decision she made. They just wanted to talk it all through, to make sure she was taking this decision for the right reasons.

Sophie, though she rolled her eyes over the phone at him, knew that she would have to face her mother at some point.

"Alright, Dad. Is Thursday night good?"
Sophie stepped into the living room, feeling like a guest in her own home. Which was silly, she knew, after only 46 days. James had opened the door for her and rushed back into the kitchen mumbling about oven temperatures. April was still upstairs and even though Sophie needed to pick up some things from her old bedroom, she waited. Waited, restless and edgy and stupidly hopeful. She reminded herself that she was well within her rights to make this decision. It was her life and her music, to give up and give away. She needed to be confident, to show her parents that she had thought this through.

"Soph, it's good to see you." April's voice preceded her. She was less put-together than usual and that surprised

Sophie. When was the last time she remembered her mother with her hair hastily tied back in a bun? But it seemed like a sort of mask had slipped from her face. There was no doubt about it; April Summers was vulnerable, and she didn't care if her daughter knew that.

Sophie got up from the sofa and crossed the distance between them, something compelling her that she couldn't put a finger on. Here was her mother, her eyes tired, every line of her suggesting that she had missed her daughter. They stared at each other for a beat before reaching, almost at the same time, for a hug. Awkward at first, but neither seemed to want to let go, softening and settling into something that clearly comforted both and said everything they couldn't. Not yet, at least.

James' voice broke the hug. He stood at the door of the living room, two half-filled glasses of wine in either hand.

"I thought you might want these now."

He handed them a glass each and walked back into the kitchen, humming a snatch of song in his absent-minded off-key way. Sophie went back to her place on the sofa, while April settled in a chair opposite. Their eyes briefly acknowledged each other as they made a silent toast. Sophie wondered what her mother had wished for and whether it was the same as her's. April was the one to break the silence.

"So, how are you doing? Am I allowed to ask?" There was none of the argumentative, hurt feeling that always raised Sophie's hackles. Instead, there was concern. It was a genuine question.

"I'm alright…" Sophie stopped, almost about to tell her about James' loan. She couldn't tell April that yet. So, she began again. 'I found a great little studio close to Lia's. The landlady lives on the ground floor. You'd like her. She's feisty, very no-nonsense but caring.' Sophie hoped her words implied that April resembled Janie. Then, she offered, emboldened by the smile that tugged at April's mouth, "You should come and see the place, once I move in."

"I'm very happy for you. We both are," April paused, measuring and considering her next words, "but you can see why we worry, why we would like to know the reason behind your decision to not play professionally."

Sophie had expected this question and was prepared with an answer that she hoped was truthful enough without getting too close to the real thing. Her parents didn't know the details of what had happened between her and Paul; only that they had mutually decided to move on. They'd liked him the times they had met, but didn't want to intrude until Sophie felt comfortable telling them, *if* she did. She took a surreptitious breath to steady herself.

"I understand the concerns, I really do. But, I just need some time away to figure things out and then I may come back to this a year or two down the line. But right now…" she trailed off and looked up at April, realising that all this while, she had been staring at the rim of her wine glass, her finger tracing and retracing a semicircle. She took a breath and launched into the part of the explanation she knew would reassure her parents.

"Mum, I want to try teaching. I always felt it was something that I'd like to do, something I might even be good at, and I want to give it a proper go. I've already got a prospective student. Janie knew some people and I'm meeting with the boy and his family later this week. I'm also composing and arranging for a lot of interesting projects." She'd said what she had been practising in front of Lia's bedroom mirror the past few days. Now, for another sip of wine, and to wait for April's reaction.

"I never realised you felt so strongly about teaching. But, of course, we support the decision, I think it's great you're branching out and trying to figure out what you really want. It's smart and brave." The last part slipped out before her mother even realised what she was saying, Sophie could tell by the way April's face rearranged itself, folding away the vulnerability. By the time James came back into the room to tell them that the lasagne was ready, her mother was April Summers again.

*

The morning following her fight with Robby, Sophie invited her mother over for a cup of tea before she could talk herself out of it. She'd picked up the phone multiple times to call her best friend but couldn't bring herself to press dial. None of their previous fights had felt like this, like she couldn't think about any of it without feeling physical pain. How could she face Robby until she fixed everything?

There was a time when Sophie yearned for sadness, for a reason for angst and anger, anything that would help her feel like she had a reason for her art, her music, like she wasn't just another well-adjusted kid from a stable, financially secure family. Now, she seemed to have made her peace with being who she was, but wanted happiness too, on top of everything? That's what Sophie was thinking of, only half listening to what her mother was saying. There had been a look about April from the moment she'd stepped over the uneven threshold into Sophie's studio. It had taken Sophie until the tea finished steeping to realise that April was nervous and that meant James had probably said something. She'd never seen her mother like this and it made her awkward.

Then the words tumbled out of them both, tripping the other up, splayed in their haste to be finally, irrevocably heard.

"I don't resent you, Sophie, how could you ever think...?

" I overheard a conversation at one of the Summers' parties, that you stopped playing because you had me, *I* was the reason. I didn't want it to be true, so I never asked you about it. But I believed it was." Sophie swallowed, her hands gripping her mug. "Why else would you not teach me yourself? Why else would you distance yourself from my music?"

That's when she realised that her words, though rubbed smooth over the years of polishing them into some semblance of perfection, were no less piercing.

April paled then flushed. "How could I ever hate you?" Not waiting for an answer, she continued, filling the space

42

with words Sophie had always longed to hear. "If anything, you my dear Soph, you gave me the break that I needed. There were, are, days when I feel like I will go crazy if I stop playing, even if it's just for myself…that I will have to keep playing and I'll be found dead with a violin in my hand." April paused. "Not the worst thing I can think of as these things go." Another pause that was softer, more hesitant. "But I never wanted everything else that came with it—being away from James, then you, the competition, the pressures—and you gave me the strength to make that decision. What I'm trying to say is, I understand more than you think I do, though your reasons might be different." The silence added *and you've never really told me.*

"Then why didn't you say something, anything? Don't you…? Sophie was unable to continue, wasn't even sure what she wanted to say.

"Would you have believed me? You seemed to be so much at odds with me."

"You never even gave yourself a chance, Mum." Sophie's voice broke.

"I spent four years listening to other people, my own parents among them; I listened to them tell me what I should do. I didn't want you to have to go through that, even by accident."

"I wanted you to, I don't know...I guess I wanted you to care."

"I've always cared, Soph. It's just that my mother was too involved in every single aspect of my life. I wanted to give you the option to make up your own mind."

Sophie wouldn't look directly at her, her eyes, instead, focused on the fine scratches at the edge of the table, her fingers lightly tracing imaginary circles. She thought again about how little they had allowed the other to know them.

"You were six years old the first time I realised how easy it would be for me to nudge you in the direction I wanted. Though in a few years you did exactly what you wanted. You were always so stubborn." A small smile shifted her features. "I'm afraid that is one thing I did pass on."

"By the time you moved out, I had convinced myself that it was too late and that me offering any advice would just make it worse. I didn't want to cloud your judgment even further. And you'd just broken up with Paul, which, well..." April delicately trailed off.

"He's...I've been meaning to tell you. He sent me an invite. They're playing at the Wigmore in a few weeks. He asked if I wanted to meet after." The words slipped out, seemingly waiting for a response, though Sophie's face suggested otherwise.

April looked like she had questions and some answers, but she waited.

"I'm not really sure whether I want to go. The last time I saw him wasn't the happiest, but what break-up conversation is? I'm not sure I want to get into it again...if it'll help."

"You never…" April paused before restarting. "We never really talked about what happened with you two. Maybe it will help me to understand better."

For two years, Sophie had wanted to tell April but now she didn't know where to start. She discarded a few options before settling on "We wanted different things" which was true enough. She sipped her tea and looked up again. "He, well, he cared about me, about my music. He wasn't afraid to show it." The accusation floated between them, though Sophie hadn't really meant it, not this time.

"But?"

"But it wasn't fair of me to expect so much from one person." As she said the words out loud for the first time, Sophie realised that she was accepting her share of the blame. There was a clarity to her thoughts and emotions that was new. It hadn't come all at once, this rushing sense of understanding; it was sneaky and slow and had obviously planned its ambush patiently. But now that it was here, she couldn't stop talking. "I always felt like I wasn't good enough.

46

How could I be when my own mother didn't trust me? Paul, he never made me feel like anything was beyond me. When he said he couldn't do it anymore, I lost even that, and I broke it off. He tried to tell me that we could work it out, that I only needed to talk to you, really talk to you. At the time everything seemed unsurmountable.'

"I never wanted to hurt you, Soph…" April's face finally crumpled, just a little. She looked away before forcing herself to look back at her daughter. "I thought I was doing what was best."

"For you or for me?" Sophie kept her voice low, still staring at the table.

"I guess I messed things up anyway." She reached a tentative hand and let it settle on Sophie's. "I'm here now, though."

The whisper settled into the fine, thready lines of her living room table and Sophie kept finding it long after she'd said goodbye to April that afternoon.

*

47

Sophie stood, flanked by green, the shrine rising tall in front of her. It seemed to be peak time, but the easy chatter was hushed in the sanctity of these grounds, making the cello at the edges of her mind stand out. She blinked and found herself suddenly by the sacred camphor tree, where people tied wooden tablets in the hope that their wishes could be heard and come true.

She closed her eyes and prayed for the right answer.

The light came in through the gauzy curtains and pooled where Sophie lay, curled up on her left side. Her eyes were closed, as if she could slip back into her dream. But she heard London getting ready for another day. She opened her eyes and rolled over to the other side, the micro webs of her dream clinging to her like fairy dust.

At least there were no traces of Robby in those fast-disappearing wisps like the last few weeks. Like the time she and Robby had spent the better part of a weekend working on his Moon Landing Lego set, celebrating with homemade lemonade and redcurrant muffins against the backdrop of the resplendent space shuttle that *they* had made. Or the summer day their parents had met at her house for dinner and the kids were allowed to stay up late, and Robby and Sophie had taken full advantage of this by dragging her tent out into the backyard and lying on their stomachs until their eyes closed into slits; she remembered being half on the blanket in the tent and half out on the grass that tickled her nose and made her sneeze.

Sophie had convinced herself that both of them needed time, when it was just her--and it's not like he'd called? -- but he'd popped up in her thoughts that week far more than she would like to admit. She also knew her mind was distracting her from one of her problems with another, especially when she was about to do something with no way of knowing if it was a good idea.

With that thought, Sophie got out of bed, slid into her dressing gown, and walked over to the kettle. She would need multiple cups of strong tea to get her through today.

*

"Miss W, how come you aren't a celebrity?"

Only Andy could tune his violin and ask inappropriate questions at the same time. He was tiny for his age and even his small violin looked two sizes too big on him. However, all that was forgotten once he started playing. He'd been playing since he was five and was among the most gifted of the kids Sophie worked with.

"Andy, how many times have I asked you not to call me Miss W?"

"But she is famous, Andy."

Lily, ever the loyal darling of the group. She was a precocious nine year old who was unusually musical for someone who'd been playing for only a few months. She was a quick and eager learner and a pleasure to teach. The opposite of Andy, who despite all his ability had the attention span of a gnat. Sophie consistently struggled to think of creative ways to make him concentrate.

"Well, I don't care either way. I like her whether she is famous or not."

Brian, her first ever student, had the last word as usual. The twelve year old was very forthcoming and refreshingly frank, something that translated into an open sweetness in his playing. He was not naturally gifted like Lily and Andy, but whatever he lacked in inherent musicality, he made up for in sheer effort, practice and sincerity.

Sophie had to smile against her better judgment. She went around the room, which was always a bit of a tough task because of how small it was, even more with three music stands to navigate. She paused at the side table near the door and leaned against it, eyes closed and concentrating on the rhythm of the arpeggios. Another was fighting for her attention. Paul's cello still tugging away at any stray thoughts. She opened her eyes to find Lily, Andy and Brian looking at her, with that almost disconcerting steady gaze children possess.

"Miss W, are you okay?"

She could have sworn Andy did it on purpose. But it made her smile.

"You ready to start what we practised last week?"

Brian smiled in that quiet way of his and for one brief moment Sophie was reminded yet again why she loved teaching.

Bach Minuet in G. Sophie had transposed the harmonies for a trio and they walked through the parts which needed most work. It was amazing how far they had come with the piece, their playing disjointed and raw yet more linked than previous weeks.

Later, Sophie was explaining what they should prepare for the following week, when her phone made a deep rumbling sound against the wood of the windowpane. All three of them were packing up their instruments and looked up. "The vibration always makes me feel jittery, like the sound of nails across a blackboard," Brian said matter of factly the first time it happened, and the other two had agreed. At least her phone got them to agree on something.

Going over to Lydia's later. You sure you don't want to come? Mum x

Sophie ignored the cramp of guilt and walked her students to the door.

*

Wigmore Hall was only a short walk from Oxford Street, but it seemed like Sophie was walking for miles. She was glad she had talked herself out of wearing heels and gone for strappy flat sandals instead, but her feet automatically slowed down as she came closer to the distinctive glass canopy at the entrance, flanked by two white intricately carved marble pillars. She had played there only once, a few years ago, but she knew it with her eyes closed. April's own quartet had been a Wigmore favourite. Sophie was determined not to think about that. Tonight was hard enough as it was.

Looking around inside, she realised that there were a few familiar faces. Sophie pretended she'd received an urgent phone call and went over to the far corner of the lobby. She regretted it as soon as she turned to her left and saw the poster. His hair was a bit longer in the photo. But everything else was the same. She forced herself to look away at the side and read the concert programme. The Cantoni Quartet were starting off with Beethoven's *String Quartet No. 16,* followed by Mendelssohn's *String Quartet No. 6,* and after the interval, finishing off with *String Quartet No. 14 in D Minor* by Schubert. Lingering loss and death. Sophie was glad when everyone was allowed to go in.

Not much had changed after the renovation. The same rectangular hall with a small stage raised at the end, renaissance style alabaster and marble walls, and the cupola. The cupola was a source of fascination that had strengthened after she read the history behind it. The Soul of Music gazing up at the Genius of Harmony with his ball of eternal fire reflecting rays across the world. The deep blue sky with the Divine Mystery. An intricate pattern of thorns separating them from the rest of the painting represented the physical separation of humanity from the "perfect spiritual conception of music" because of their attachment to materialism.

Sophie sat down in her seat. Her eyes caught the same poster, on both sides of the stage. She gave a little start as someone tapped her shoulder. The man who had brought her out of her thoughts and the woman with him were in the seats to Sophie's right. She stood up and let them pass, still dazed. By the time she had settled down again, the curtain had risen, and she could hear familiar sounds. Then there he was. She couldn't see his eyes but wondered whether he would be looking out for her, to see if she actually came. The first line of the music put that out of her mind.

*

For the twenty-five odd minutes of the Mendelssohn, Sophie felt herself close enough to touch the music, the bitter-sweet emotions that Mendelssohn had infused into the last major composition he wrote before his passing two months later. A tribute after the death of his sister, Fanny. A personal goodbye that could be anyone's version of their own. Sophie closed her eyes to stop the tears, eyes pressed close. Paul's cello was everywhere, even when he was sustaining long notes or soft harmonies, forming the bassline against which the entire

Cantoni rested. He was their stable foundation to build upon. She missed him.

During the interval, Sophie looked forward to the Schubert in the same way a person who knows the ending of a sad film still looks forward to the journey. When the curtain finally went up and she saw Paul make his way onto the stage with the others, Sophie found that her heart was beating rapidly, tears already pressing at the backs of her eyes. *Death and the Maiden*. Schubert's testament to the death he realised that he couldn't escape. The first time Sophie had heard it, she had visualised the sharp changes between the pace and the melodies as extreme contrasts of colour in a painting.

The intricate polyphony now allowed each instrument in the Cantoni to infuse its own voice, its own unique personality. Layers upon layers to form a rich complex tapestry that Sophie found herself getting entangled in. The furious, violent nature of composition and rhythms didn't help slow down her heart rate, but she felt integrated with its dark vision and unyielding foreboding of death. She felt Schubert's initial pain and terror at the thought of impending, early death, and the final resignation and acceptance of that fact.

And yet, just as none of the themes used in the four movements ever really settle, even after approaching a resolution that is ultimately snatched away, Sophie's indecision didn't reach a final resolution, each time coming within an inch of it before slipping away. Leaving her more confused than ever. She knew the ending was coming but still felt the ache as the Cantoni played the D Major, a happy, triumphant win against the odds, and suddenly shifted to the D Minor, an unresolved, tragic conclusion.

Sophie felt her remaining hope being torn away, her cheeks shiny with tears. She wasn't the only one. It had been a breath taking performance, energy and virtuosity even in the face of a theme about death. It would definitely be a part of the Wigmore Hall Live recordings. She looked at Paul; the smile was back on his face, the shy, polite one reserved for performances and critics.

Theirs was a relationship based on so much more than just music. But it did start and end with it. Sophie felt the magnetic tug in all its intensity as she stood with all the others, still clapping the Cantoni, who were but a few feet away. She was physically closer to him than she'd been in years, and yet her feet took her to the bathroom, where she found herself leaning, her palms flat on the counter. She took a few deep breaths, her mind far away, immersed in sounds.

That last summer before they parted for good, they'd fallen into the habit of playing together after dinner on the nights Sophie stayed over—simple pieces familiar since childhood and later, other more difficult ones not easily attempted, ones they grew close to in that enclosed space where the only sounds were of them playing and breathing. Where there was mirrored hesitation at any movement that might take the music a bit further away from where it loitered still within the walls of Paul's rental apartment.

Sophie looked at her reflection in the mirror and imagined herself walking down the hallway of the hotel he and the rest of the quartet were staying at, the hotel he had mentioned in the handwritten note accompanying her invitation addressed and mailed by what she assumed was his agent. *It would be nice to see you.* She imagined calling up to his room from reception, then waiting for him in the hotel bar, her shoulders thrown back, her voice steady.

Since the invite, she had practised what she'd say if she could, editing and revising as she imagined a determined writer might, until there were no rough edges. Now she realised she was mistaken. She'd pared it all away.

Sophie was soaked by the time she walked to Oxford Street, the rain hardly registering. She felt her sandals squelch down the steps of the Tube and she hoped, rather belatedly, that her phone was okay in the pocket of her peacoat. As if it knew, it began to vibrate and Sophie fumbled with it until she could see who it was. She almost let it go to voicemail, waiting for another beat before she finally tapped the green button on the screen.

There was silence on the other end of the line.

"Robby, you there?"

"Yes."

His voice sounded like it would rip if stretched any further.

"Soph, it's my mum."

*

"Feels like last week that I told you off for going over without telling me. But you were more interested in telling me all about their door knocker."

James stood just outside their open front door, Sophie in tow. April was talking to Robby on the phone in the foyer, last-minute logistical help for Mrs. Summers' wake later that day.

Sophie was surprised. She hadn't expected her father to remember that. The Summers had one of those intricately carved and polished door knockers. She had been fascinated by its slightly sinister shape of a dragon's head, but what had interested her more was the sound. It made you want to wiggle your shoulders because the echo followed you and coursed through you faster than you could lift them.

"See you soon, Robby. We're leaving for the church now." April slipped the phone in her purse and dabbed a final tissue under the eyes. Sophie's stomach clenched and unclenched.

*

On the first day of Year 2, Robby Summers was the new kid in their class of twenty. A class where everyone knew the other and they had all come up through kindergarten. He was quiet and kept to himself during all their classes before mid-morning break. But looking at him, it felt like part of his mind was somewhere far away, lost in a world where only he existed, he and his imagination. Sophie kept glancing to his side of the room, wondering what could be so interesting in the book they were assigned to read by their English teacher, Roald Dahl's *The BFG*.

As soon as the bell rang for break, Sophie gathered up her lunch and walked over to where he sat, just by the

61

window. He was still intently staring at the book, looking up only when Sophie's shadow fell across the page. He waited for her to say something.

"Hi, I'm Sophie, but you can call me Soph." She had all the disarming lack of self-consciousness special to kids.

"I'm Robby, but you can call me Spiderman."

He suddenly smiled. A wide genuine grin that lit up his blue eyes. At that moment, Sophie already felt like she'd known Robby Summers all her life.

It turned out that the Summers were their new neighbours. They were staying with friends until all their stuff could be set up. One weekend soon after they had moved in, Robby knocked on Sophie's door and asked her if she could join them for a picnic. It was a surprisingly warm day for October and the air was bracing, but not so much that the tip of her nose turned red.

Even as the day unfurled, Sophie knew that there were certain details she wanted to remember when she thought about that day years from now. The delicious taste of honey-

62

roasted ham and mustard sandwiches after a game of Frisbee, the cocker spaniel who kept trying to join in their game and she was sure would be better than her at it (Robby was very good and took it easy on her), the same cocker spaniel who returned later to play catch with them, the stories she and Robby made up about what it must be like to live in Buckingham Palace, which you could see from where they were sitting. Sophie also wanted to remember how attentively Mrs. Summers listened to what she said, how seriously she answered the questions of two six year olds, no matter how silly. That was what Sophie wanted to remember most.

Now, as she walked out into the back garden and saw her best friend for the first time since their fight, it was that feeling that Sophie gathered close and around her. They had avoided looking at each other throughout the service at the church; only a brief glance when she and her parents first walked in and offered their condolences. April and James and some of their other neighbours had slipped away early to get things ready at the house for the wake. Sophie had joined them, not knowing what else to do with the energy that made her both restless and lethargic.

Robby, standing alone, gazing at one of Lydia's many plants looked tired and sad. Her own heart squeezed in her chest as he looked up at her approach across the overgrown grass.

"Robby, I'm sorry."

"I know. You've only apologised like a hundred times in the past week."

"I think it's more like eighty, but I'm serious. I'm sorry—about this, about back then, about everything."

"Everything's not your fault."

"A wise person told me to be honest, so that's what I'm doing. I messed up and I didn't even realise for how long."

"You did mess up, Soph. But not this. This…" he indicated to his childhood home and all the people gathered inside, "this is just what it is. If you need it to feel better then yes, you did wrinkle it all up a little." He looked back at the plants when he said this but both of them were smiling.

"I spoke to her...my mum, I mean. I told her I knew that she'd lied about why she stopped performing...and, well, everything else."

Robby looked at her from the corner of his eye, like he used to when they were kids and convinced that they could move their eyes into the backs of their heads.

"I think we might be okay, really okay, for, well, the first time since I was seven. But all I can think about since you called me is what your mum would have said to that."

"I told you so." They both said together, their smiles reaching their eyes for a brief moment. "I wish I could've given her the chance to say that," Soph added. Her voice wobbled then straightened itself.

Robby held out one arm.

"I already miss her, Soph."

"Me too."

Sophie closed the distance between them and leaned against him.

"Robby?"

He turned his head towards her.

"You were also right about Paul. I didn't need to see him, not really."

"How was the concert then?" The side of his mouth quirked.

Sophie laughed, feeling something levitate inside her chest for the first time in months. "Now that you ask, it was amazing. But that's all it was.'

Since the night of the concert a week ago, the cello in her head had resolved into a rigid but not unwelcome presence. She shifted and put her head on Robby's shoulder. He rested the side of his against hers, which is how April found them. In the week since Lydia passed, Sophie had spoken to her about the audition and decided to give it a chance. Who knows what microscopic steps lead us to a moment of time patiently waiting for us? As Sophie looked up, her mother's shadow by her feet, she heard them. During rambles around Shinjuku Gyoen on a summer exchange at Trinity, she had toyed with the themes of passing time layered over the memory of that moment in the city where her parents fell in love, a chance occurrence traced into the future to her existence. At the end of the trip, all she remembered was a vague sense of hope somewhere she couldn't place. Now, the melody, quiet, resolute, jumped off the edge of all things.

"I'll just tell them you needed some fresh air. Take your time." April's face spilled over with the loss of her own best friend, but her gaze held Sophie's for a long moment before she walked back into the house, as if sensing that her daughter always envisioned two violins even if Sophie's realisation had just nudged in.

The back door closed with a soft sucking in of air and then there was silence, as Sophie and Robby turned back around and watched his late mother's favourite plants until it was time to go back inside.

Acknowledgements:

To the family that has always supported and believed in me and my work (including offering some very constructive criticism).

A big thank you to my parents for the love, for never forcing me to choose a different profession despite three surgeons and two doctors in the family, for allowing me to be who I am.

To my dad for the introduction to the magical world of words and languages.

To my mum, for everything. Now and always.

To my brilliant sister, Anju, with whom I made up my first stories, shared (and still share) my favourite books, to my cousins-like-sisters Sanjana and Shivani for all the nerdiness and laughs and yolos (a special shoutout to Shivani for designing the perfect cover; this book is even closer to my heart because we got to work together on it—to many more!). To all three for trusting that this story would one day be finished and be worth telling.

To Seema Maushi, Vasanti Maushi, and Shailu Mama, the coolest aunts and uncle ever, for the laughs and the love. Vasanti Maushi, thank you, also, for the music and the artistic inspiration and insight. I've tried to write this story with those sensibilities.

To friends who give me faith when mine wavers and laughter when I need it (and all the memes and witty banter), no matter geographical distance or time zones; you know who you are.

To the late Jo Powell, a fantastic tutor, who read the earliest iteration of this story and encouraged me to further explore it, with her insights and her enthusiasm.

To Robert Sheppard, for guiding me through the intense year that was my master's and the many versions this story went through over those 8 months; for the feedback and the continuing belief in Sophie and her story.

To my other writing tutors at Edge Hill—Ailsa Cox (your blurb for this means the world; thank you for teaching me to love the short story form— I've learned so much from you), Dan Pantano (thank you for always championing me and my work, for your friendship, and for introducing me to the wonderful possibilities of poetry), and Andrew Oldham (*L'effet de Papillon* was where it all began, and I'll always be grateful to you for being the first publisher to take a chance on my work, for your support and faith ever since).

To Kirsten Schlewitz, editor extraordinaire, for the keen eye, the ability to understand exactly what I want to say and to help me say it to the best of my skills, always. Jellyfishes for life!

To Marie Hebert and Felix Herbst for the valuable inputs about the classical music world—any remaining errors are my own—thank you for sharing your expertise so that I could ensure as much musical authenticity as possible.

To Lauren O'Mara who helped me brainstorm certain London locations when I didn't know where to start—I love that you're a part of this story that takes place in the city that has seen so many of our best memories (and many more to come).

To Sarthak Dev and Piyush Bisht, my novelette beta readers, for the helpful comments and the love and support.

To Beverley Lee, my friend and bestselling author, for the lovely blurb.

To Red and Alien Buddha Press for this opportunity to share my work with the world.

And finally, but far from the least, to all of you who've ever read or shared or loved my work, who have written reviews and sent messages of support or excitement—it means more than I can say, or write about (yes, yes, I know!).

About the Author:

Hope is **Anushree "Anu" Nande's** superpower. Arsenal Football Club, perhaps irrationally, dominates many of her waking (and sleeping) hours; the rest she spends reading, writing, editing hoarding books, working through creative demons with sport and art, and asking herself what Coach Taylor would do.

She is a Mumbai-born writer who has studied and worked in the United Kingdom, Spain and the United States, and is currently a senior team member at Football Paradise, an award-winning website for longform articles about football, and a freelance editor and publishing professional. Her microfiction collection, *55 Words*, was published by Underground Voices in 2015 and her other work (fiction, essays, football pieces, poetry) can be found in a range of online and print platforms. Anushree's writing, in whatever form, tends to explore how we navigate the emotional landscape of our lives, and is always hopeful.

Printed in Great Britain
by Amazon